Clifford's Valentines

Library of Congress Cataloging-in-Publication Data is available.

ISBN-13: 978-0-439-18300-0
ISBN-10: 0-439-18300-6

28 27 26 25 24 13 14 15 16/0

Printed in the U.S.A. 40 • This edition first printing, August 2008

BEGINNING READER LEVEL 1 50-250 WORDS

NORMAN BRIDWELL

Clifford's Valentines

Cartwheel BOOKS®

SCHOLASTIC INC.
New York Toronto London Auckland Sydney
Mexico City New Delhi Hong Kong Buenos Aires

It is Valentine's Day.

BE
MINE

Clifford gets a card.
It is from a boy.

Clifford gets a card.
It is from a girl.

Clifford gets a card
from a woman.

Clifford gets a card
from a man.

The letter carrier comes.

CLIFFORD

CLIFFORD

Now Clifford gets many, many more cards.
Everyone loves Clifford!

It starts to snow.

CLIFFORD

It snows and snows.
Clifford has an idea.

He runs to the park.

The boy, the girl, the woman,
and the man are there.

Many, many other people are there, too.

Clifford makes a heart in the snow.

Happy Valentine's Day, everyone!

• Word List •

a
an
and
are
boy
card
carrier
Clifford
comes
day
everyone
from
gets
girl
happy
has
heart
idea
in
is
it
letter
loves
makes
man
many
more
now
other
park
people
runs
snow
starts
the
there
to
too
Valentine's
woman